Merry Christmas, Mom
Love,
'98

D1164983

First edition 1998

Library of Congress Cataloging-in-Publication Data

Rosen, Michael J., date.
The dog who walked with God / Michael J. Rosen ;
illustrated by Stan Fellows. — 1st U.S. ed.
p.   cm.
Summary: A Kato creation story in which our familiar world
emerges from an empty, dark, and watery place so lonely that even
the Creator needed a companion before setting foot there.
ISBN 0-7636-0470-4
1. Kato Indians—Folklore. 2. Tales—California.
[1. Creation—Folklore. 2. Kato Indians—Folklore. 3. Indians of
North America—California—Folklore. 4. Folklore—California.]
I. Fellows, Stanley, date, ill. II. Title.
E99.K267R68   1998
398.2'08997—dc21   97-27710

10 9 8 7 6 5 4 3 2 1

Printed in Belgium

This book was typeset in M Perpetua.
The pictures were done in watercolor and pencil.
Calligraphy by Nancy Ruth Leavitt, Stillwater, Maine

Candlewick Press
2067 Massachusetts Avenue
Cambridge, Massachusetts 02140

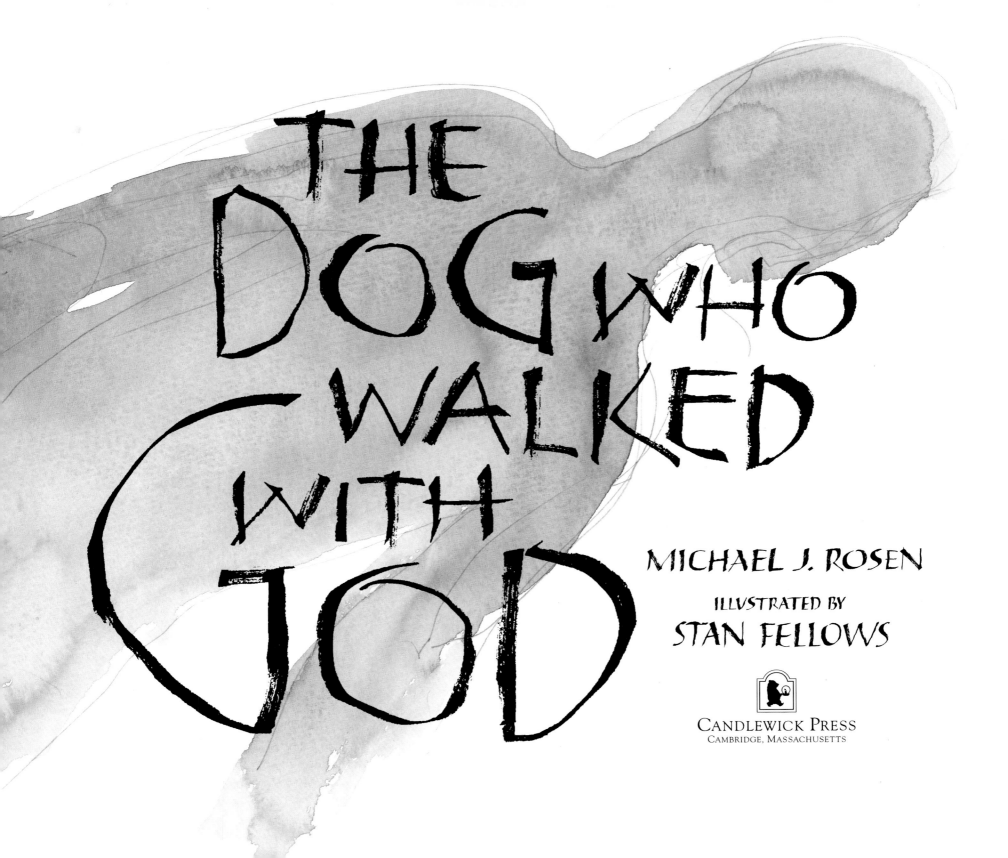

THE DOG WHO WALKED WITH GOD

MICHAEL J. ROSEN

ILLUSTRATED BY
STAN FELLOWS

CANDLEWICK PRESS
CAMBRIDGE, MASSACHUSETTS

WATER, THEY SAY, WAS EVERYWHERE

and land was not.

Mountains were not,

and stones were not.

And neither were there trees

or grass or fish or deer

or grizzlies or wolves.

People, too, had all been washed away, they say,

along with all these animals of every kind.

ONLY WATER LIVED ANYWHERE.

Owls and buzzards were lost to the earth.
No heron flew across the water,
        no quail or jay or screech owl.
No oriole or meadowlark or sparrow hawk
        perched anywhere;
        nowhere was there a place to perch.
No pelican or duck dove toward the water.

Gone from the world, they say,
were foxes and wildcats,
        otters and minks,
                jackrabbits and elk.
        No squirrel, they say—
        not a gray or a red or a ground squirrel—
lived anywhere
among the water that was all.

GREAT BLUE HERON

MINK

WESTERN MEADOWLARK

RED FOX

Even wind was nowhere, they say.
No snow. No frost.
        No rain. No thunder
                or fog or lightning or clouds or stars.
It was dark, they say. All dark.

The sun itself was nowhere
        when Earth rose up at last and stood,
                its head above the water, the water
                        snug around its shoulders.

In shallow places where Earth looked up,
 moss grew, they say,
  and Earth grew taller,
and onto it stepped
 the Great Traveler and his companion.

Where horns of Earth rose high,
 he mounded grayish clay.
White reeds and blue grasses he placed there,
 and trees, trees he made stand up.

"I am finishing," he said, they say,
 and soon a mountain became
   a somewhere from the everywhere
 that was water, and the water
 broke against it.

Bushes and underbrush he set upon the mountain,
    and small stones, which would grow large.
"I am fixing it," the Great Traveler said, they say.
    "I will go north, and fix the earth."
        And from above, he and his companion
        set to fixing all.

And when he heard
      the thunder, they say, the old thunder
      of the rocks, he piled the tall rocks
      high in the south   and in the west
          and in the north   and in the east.
Pillars of rocks he piled, they say,
      to fix the sky
      forever above the earth.

For clouds,

> he made a great hole in the sky
> so they could travel here and beyond.

And for fog,

> he made a second hole
> so it could wander here and beyond.

For dew, they say,

> he made a fire in the water.

And as for thunder,

> he told it live, they say, live
> high above in another world.

Then from the ground,
the Great Traveler made a man.
"To him, I will talk," he said, they say.
A leg, left and right;
an arm, left and right.
For a stomach, he gathered grass.
Heart and liver, lungs and mouth—
he made each part, they say,

and he made a woman, too.

For them,
he let the wind blow,
he let the sky rain,
he let the fog come in.

"For what shall I make the sun?"
he said, they say, and he decided
fire, for heat.

"For what shall I make the moon?"
he said, they say, and he decided
night, for cold.

And as it rained and rained,
the Great Traveler wondered
what should swim in the water,
and so he set loose creatures there:
bull snake became   black salmon,
salamander became   hook-bill,
grass snake became   steelhead,
lizard became   trout.

He wondered then
what should take root
in all this water,
and he made seaweed, they say,
and abalone,   mussels,
kelp,   and blue grasses.

AMBERJACK

TIGER-SALAMANDER

Salt he brought from the foam of ocean,
    and soon the first waves rose skyward
and settled back again, this time
    on the sand that was waiting there for them.

Sea lions crawled ashore,
    whales dove deeper out to sea,
      and devilfish,
      which are ugly but good to eat,
      swam within reach.
"It will be good," he said, they say.
    "So many fishes will swim the sea."

MUSSEL

SPERM WHALE

FIDDLER CRAB

Along the shore
    he planted fir trees and redwoods,
    chestnuts and tan oaks,
which all grew large.
Yellow pines he lined up by the water
    and stepped back to see that they were growing.
One by one—white oaks,
    black oaks, sugar pines—
he raised the forests of the world.

Then scraping his foot across the land,
    the Great Traveler made a creek.
"Here the water will be good," he said, they say.
    "Not salty, like the ocean water."
And fresh water filled his tracks
    so that the panther
        and the elk could drink
    and so the ravens and the gray squirrels—
    all the creatures could drink.
"Here, drink the water," he told his dog,
    the dog who, from the beginning,
    had walked beside the Great Traveler.
"I, too, will drink.
    And grizzlies will drink,
    and people will drink."

TAMARACK

WHITE OAK LEAF

AMERICAN CHESTNUT

GRIZZLY

ELK

RAVEN

Into this sweet water, then, the Great Traveler
  released the salamander and the turtle.
He loosed the small fish and the crawfish,
  the eel, steelhead, and salmon.
"And onto the mountain," he said, they say,
  "panthers will be many,
    and jackrabbits, many,
      and deer, many as well."
He made the blue flies and the wasps.
  He made the yellow jackets, too,
  although he did not like them,
  and almost killed them all.
And everywhere his dog walked with him.

ARMADILLO

BIG HORN
SHEEP

PRONGHORN

CARIBOU

PAINTED TURTLE

SPINY SOFTSHELL

SUNFISH

NORTHERN LEOPARD FROG

CHUM SALMON

Along the streams and creeks they walked,
and the Great Traveler made the brush
climb up the mountain.
Manzanita and whitethorn he placed into a valley.
"Grizzlies will be many," he said, they say,
"and rattlesnakes, many.
The land will be good." And there he made
the barking owl, screech owl,
little owl, and grosbeak.

"Birds will be many,"
        he said, they say:
blue jays and grouse
        and quail and robins
and woodcocks and yellowhammers
        and mockingbirds
and meadowlarks and blackbirds
        and kingfishers,
        who will catch fish,
and buzzards and ravens
        and chicken hawks, too.

YELLOW-HEADED BLACKBIRD

REDHEADED
WOODPECKER

RUFFED GROUSE

WOODCOCK

"Now let it hail,

let clouds come now," he said, they say.

"Let rains cause the streams to rise

and the mud to appear."

And the Great Traveler circled back

to watch for each of his created things to grow.

GRAY FOX

BADGER

CHOKEBERRY

"My dog, come look," he said, they say.
    And anywhere they turned, the new green
        spread into the bushes and trees.
           Fish filled every brimming creek.
        Rocks stretched higher into a range of mountains.
In the valleys, his creatures leaped
      and flew and galloped and swam.
All Earth had become good.

And so the Great Traveler went back, they say,
with his dog. "Walk fast, my dog.
        The mountains have grown taller,
        the land has grown fertile.
        The water is flowing with trout.
It is warm here and the earth is good."

And grizzlies and rattlesnakes
        and turtles and deer
and all the animals he had promised
would be many were many indeed.
"Walk fast, my dog," he said, they say.
        "The land, we've made it good, my dog."

Chestnuts ripened. Hazelnuts fell from the trees.
The berries of the manzanita whitened.
Buckeyes blossomed, peppernuts blackened,
and grasses flowered
in the north   and the south
and the east   and the west.
From each of their footsteps, grasshoppers sprang.
"My dog, we made it good," he said, they say.
"There is everywhere something
wonderful to eat."

"Drink the water again,
        my dog," he said, they say.
"We are going back now. We are near."
And the Great Traveler and his dog
        retraced their steps
        across the good growing world
        they had created.
"We are almost there, my dog," he said, they say.
        And across the valleys
        and mountains and creeks
            they walked toward the north,
            from where he and his dog
            had first stepped into a world
            so empty
        it could not have been imagined
        without the company of a dog.

"We made it good, my dog,"
        the Great Traveler said, they say.
And the two travelers walked back
        toward the horizon, leaving Earth
        to us, everywhere fixed,
        everything grown
        and still growing.

The Kato Indians were a small group of Athapaskan peoples who inhabited the valleys of northern California. In 1906, anthropologist Pliny Earle Goddard recorded the words of one of the few remaining Kato, a man in his sixties named Bill Ray, who shared a cluster of myths and tales in both his own language and in English. I wish I were able to translate directly from the lost language of this lost people, but I do hope to have captured the sounds of this one man's recollected myths, their pace and accumulating rhythm. For example, Bill Ray's tale in English begins: "Water went, they say. Waters well met, they say. Land was not, they say. Water only then, mountains were not, they say. Stones were not, they say." I also hope to have preserved two other things that impressed me in all my readings within these tales: First, the Kato's reverence for the world's nearly unaccountable richness, in which every species possesses both a name and a need to be called by it. And second, the Kato's love for their dogs. They gave these animals special names, housed them indoors at night, and buried them just as they did their own people. A dog was so much a part of their world, they even believed their creator had to have such a companion as he undertook the difficult making of a world of goodness out of emptiness.

For many of us, the world is still that new, still empty in places, and still inconceivable without the company of a dog. And so it is to those fellow dog people that this story is dedicated.

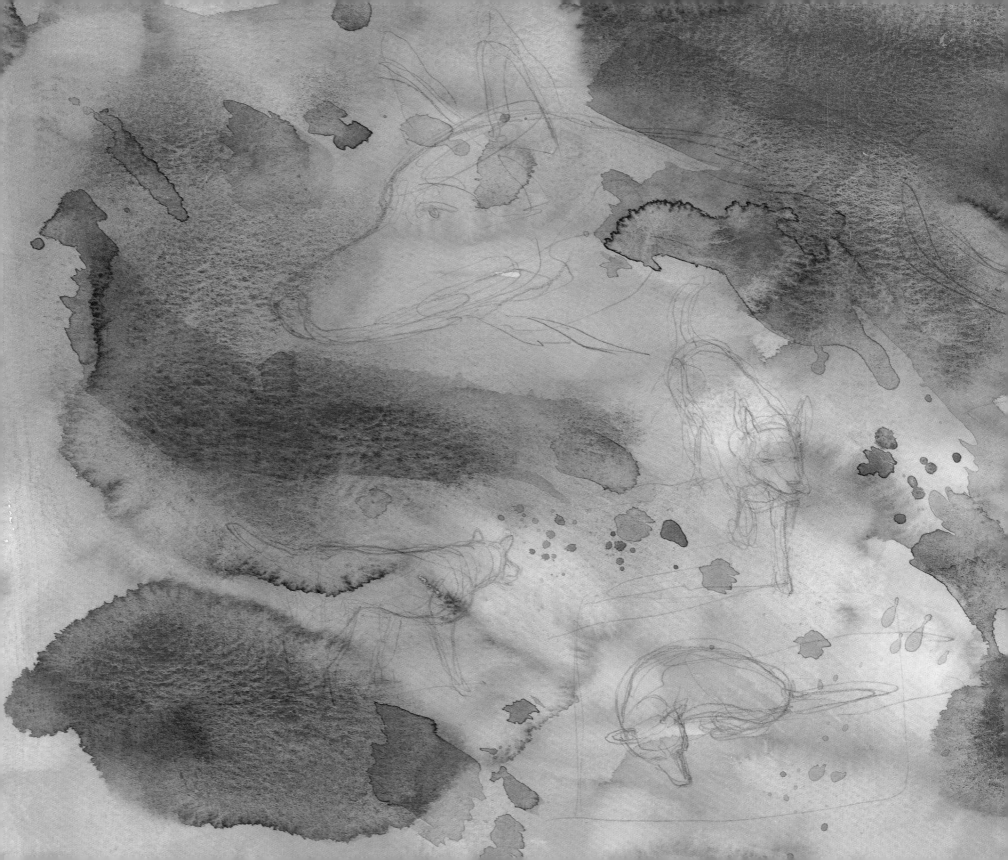